For Mom—M. B.
For David Christiana—A. R.

SIMON & SCHUSTER BOOKS FOR YOUNG READERS
An imprint of Simon & Schuster Children's Publishing Division
1230 Avenue of the Americas, New York, New York 10020
Text copyright © 2009 by Mac Barnett
Illustrations copyright © 2009 by Adam Rex
SIMON & SCHUSTER BOOKS FOR YOUNG READERS is a trademark of Simon & Schuster, Inc.
Book design by Lucy Ruth Cummins
The text for this book is set in Graham.
The illustrations for this book are rendered in gouache and mixed media.
Manufactured in China
10 9 8 7 6 5 4 3 2
Library of Congress Cataloging-in-Publication Data
Barnett, Mac.
Guess again! / Mac Barnett ; illustrated by Adam Rex.—1st ed.
p. cm.
ISBN: 978-1-4169-5566-5 (alk. paper)
1. Children's poetry, American. I. Rex, Adam, ill. II. Title.
PS3602.A83427G84 2009
811′.6—dc22
2008012882
1109 SCP

Guess Again!

written by
Mac Barnett

illustrated by
Adam Rex

Simon & Schuster Books for Young Readers
New York London Toronto Sydney

He steals carrots from the neighbor's yard.
His hair is soft, his teeth are hard.
His floppy ears are long and funny.
Can you guess who? That's right! My

Grandpa Ned.

ho's on Captain Gluebeard's shoulder?
Gold is gold. That feather's golder.
Got a guess? It's time to share it.
It's Polly! She's the pirate's

Their fleece is warm and woolly white.
And when you lie awake at night,
Count them and you'll fall asleep.
A guess? Why, yes! A flock of

He's always getting stuck in trees.
My grandma says he makes her sneeze.
He's got long whiskers and—what's that?
Why, yes! You've guessed it! It's my

Grandpa Ned.

Who's furry, scurries, and has fleas?
Who climbs our counters and eats our cheese?
We've set up traps all through the house
But still can't catch that pesky

Viking.

ho's got white teeth and fiery breath
And scares Sir Frank the Brave to death?
This frightened knight must stop his braggin'.
Who's spooked our knight? That's right! A

ho growls and has a lot of hair?

Who naps and—wait! That's not a bear!

He'll crash your picnic, steal your bread.

But it's no bear! It's Grandpa

Alan.